Forgotten Kaleidoscopes

Forgotten Kaleidoscopes

Poems
by

Deepa Agarwal

AUTHORSPRESS

Worldwide Circulation through Authorspress Global Network
First Published in 2021
by
Authorspress
Q-2A Hauz Khas Enclave, New Delhi-110 016 (India)
Phone: (0) 9818049852
E-mail: authorspressgroup@gmail.com
Website: www.authorspressbooks.com

Forgotten Kaleidoscopes
(Poems)

ISBN 978-93-91314-12-5

Printed in India at Thomson Press (India) Limited

Dedication

To All Poets Struggling to be Heard

Contents

Womanspeak

Forgotten Kaleidoscopes

Cunningly,
colours will sneak past the corner of your eye
and stun it into stillness. Arch into hopeful rainbows
gleam like a palette of gems
scattered by a scheming jeweller.

Cunningly, they will wipe themselves out
like a whimsical kaleidoscope
in a child's hands.

Who smashed
all these glass bangles and
poured the shards into a cylinder
to entertain a child?
who planned the glittering patterns,
that shifted before my spellbound eyes.

Were they gathered from frenzied wrists shedding colour?
because a woman's life must lose colour
without a man; no matter
how many indifferent rainbows stain the sky.

Dressing for Papa's funeral
in a white sari, my Christian mother asks
what shall I do with these bangles?
four red glass bangles
that absent mindedly adorned her wrists.
Break them, says her matter-of-fact friend.

A Tale of Two Princesses

Once there was a princess, who wept pearls,
and once there was a princess
who laughed flowers. Both died, I heard.
One of weeping
and the other of laughter.
But not because one's eyes went dry
or the other forgot how to laugh.
One died of suffocation
entombed in pearls. The other choked
on a surfeit of flowers.
The pearls were sold for a fortune, I heard.
But the wilted flowers brought no gain at all.
Since then, I have heard
A woman's tears have become
far more precious than her laughter.

This is Not a Country with Smooth Roads

This is not a country with smooth roads
or safe ones.
We have always known
haven't we?
As we jolt along
grateful to arrive at our destination
whole, intact.

This is no country for women
young or old.
And every day that knowledge is reinforced
when the headlines shout.

Four men raped, brutalised two women
on the road last night
while phone cameras whirred
and shame rode the air like an epidemic
flashing on screens
large and small.

This is no country for women
because so many claimed
it was not violence or a violation
not a crime nor defilement
but mere roadside entertainment.

She, Innocent Fly

Culture weights her back,
history and heritage
and ideals as shifting
as the mass produced spider webs that wind
around her face.

She, innocent fly,
for whom both web and cleansing broom
spell destruction

She trudges home,
embracing the wholesome medley
of a bag of groceries.

The key turns
a flame flickers
spices sizzle in burning oil
the aroma sighs
like the breath of centuries
like vapour rising from river and field
lake, mountain and ruined city.

She inhales
healing turmeric
even as chillies exude fumes
that blister her throat
and she recalls
the flower sweet breath of babes
along with the everyday reek of garbage.

Ambushed

The scent of ambush – a popular aftershave
incongruous on the face studded with nails
an arm like a noose.

The corrugated earth is a morass
that will neither protect
nor bear witness.

Sound flees
once the cudgel stops pounding
and the clouds rain blood.

The eyes that greet me turn sightless
the miasma of defeat
a permanent stalker
an odious scent fused to my skin
and the ridged earth a traitor
that will not contain or expel me
and the odious scent fused to my skin.
Forever.

Mother Dominica's Tranquil Square

In the tranquil square of memory
I play hopscotch
and master the art of throwing pebbles
accurately into the right space.
one-legged, I negotiate the trickery
of dividing lines
and cloister my small defeats
as deep as the shrapnel
a pink-faced nun
has sequestered somewhere.

All has been quiet on the Western front
for long now
its silence
contained in the incomplete square
whose corners frame
the tranquil face
that has interred
a mammoth
with such apparent ease
in a subterranean grotto
far removed from Mother Mary's
benign gaze.

a mammoth moving
on an abandoned chequerboard
constantly playing and replaying
a long surrendered game.

Till a friendly conversation about cats
blasts away the ice
and another square reveals itself.
A grave
tenanted with a
frozen block of memory
that unexpectedly vaporises
in the heat of a distant land.

How easily a quisling spark
can insinuate itself
into innocent talk of cats
rout the comforting dark.
How hard to bury the memory
of a brother
who tormented cats once
and grew up to be swallowed
by Mother Russia
while fighting for the Fatherland.
How treacherous the tranquility
of the cloistered square.

Note: This poem was inspired by a phrase 'the tranquil square of memory' from Rukmini Bhaya Nair's poem 'Intimations'.

Word Limit

At one I had a vocabulary of perhaps 5 words
at sixteen, maybe 100,000.
I expended them so recklessly
that this treasure was taken away
for safekeeping
locked up like my jewellery
in a safe dark vault.

Women cannot take care of words.
Words, persistent as ghouls
rising from quicksand
enduring as diamonds
gouged from clotted blood
portentous as oracles
potent as viruses
resonant as the music of myths.

and so, I remain wordless
within my limits.

My Place in the Sun

Please do not choose my place in the sun
for me
I would rather seek it myself.
How can you tell
how bright I like my sunshine?
Whether the scorching heat
of the place that you favour
suits the texture of my soul?
Do you care
that such a high temperature blisters my heart?
The blinding glare forces my eyes shut,
parches my tongue into silence?
Maybe I don't want a place in the sun at all
Maybe I simply prefer a cool spot in the shade.

Do Not Weep Lonely Mirror

The mirror in which I sought myself once
sought me in turn, when spurned,
its emptiness grew too vast for it to face.
Emptiness, that black hole into which we must fall
each one of us. The mirror pursued me
even as I fled it
time's wrinkles embedded deep in the
coils of my being. I fled the truth
imprinted on its shining glass.
The truth of countless lies
that rustled like the fugitive wings of birds
evading the trapper,
not knowing how futile my flight. Because
the world might be large
but mirrors are everywhere. And truth,
the chameleon, finds many places to hide itself.
In the starlit eyes of a lover perhaps...
the trusting warmth of a child's palm,
the adrenaline burst of the winning post,
or the murky pool of failure. Even in
the flashing pane of a neighbour's window
or the reckless flow of your pen across a page.

I could not escape, and yet how long is it
since I have known that the face in the mirror
is not my own. Not the girl who wept in the dark
once. Or boarded a train on a winter morning,
basking in the sun's warmth.
The woman who found babes in the wood
under a coverlet of fallen leaves
or listened to the urgent summons of a conch
bellowing in the dark behind hidden doors.

Who knows where it is, the face I would call my own,
if not in the mirror that faces me?
It is enough that it exists.
Whether flowing secretly in the veins of a leaf,
blowing in the dust of a storm,
or gleaming in a sunset cloud…

So, do not weep lonely mirror
Nothing is as complete as emptiness
Nothing as loud as the silence that speaks.

Anarkali

When the walls rose up
around Anarkali
her heart unfolded
in paeans of joy
(So the movies say)
celebrating love.
Her song soared up
higher, sweeter
even as the last patch of sky
was bricked out.

Salim mourned.
But life is long
and love short.
And finally
there was consolation...
There was Noor Jehan

The slave girl
when she dared to love
little knew
that
the walls of love
press close
fatal,
they shut out the sky.

And once,
the air inside
is breathed up
nothing remains
but the song,

And even that
is often lost
scattered, dissolved
by the winds of time...

Accident Prone Women

Some women just happen to be accident prone
Unseeing,
they walk into doors and smash their faces.
Heedless,
they trip while alighting from a bus,
and end up with an arm or leg in plaster.
Incredibly,
each room in the house holds danger for them.
They slip in the bathroom and knock themselves out,
set themselves afire while cooking,
sometimes they land up in hospital,
sometimes their injuries are fatal.

Accidents will happen we are told,
even in the best of families,
because some women just happen to be accident prone.

Why are they so accident prone?
Is it a genetic defect?
Or something that happened while they were growing up?
I search in the blank eyes of an accident-prone friend,
examine the unsightly bruise
my cleaning woman is hiding under her sari.
And uncover the grim truth of a battered,
not an accident-prone woman.

Woman on the Road to Lhasa

Beneath the mask
my face melts
like a *jaggery* cake in the sun.
Mercifully,
I can see
even
as I preserve the pink of my skin.

But what's the use?
my sisters remain strangers
behind yak skin cheeks
that cannot exchange smiles
to lighten
the tyranny
of the road to Lhasa. All
blinding earth and searing sky
bleached bone and rubble
hung over a chafing saddle
feeding fleas.

Only
when night's black tent
enfolds the enemy, sun,
can I breathe. Let
chilly air soothe broiling skin
let laughter flow free…
as I shed the mask.

Hard it is for a woman
far from home. And
endless the road to Lhasa
beneath a mask.

Note: Amaury de Riencourt mentions in his book *Lost World Tibet* (published 1950) that while travelling, wealthy Tibetan women wore painted face masks of yak hide to protect their complexions from the sun. Jaggery is a kind of unrefined sugar.

Mother India

Mother India. Her shoulders are broad
her forehead high. She wishes
to spread her arms wide
and circumscribe the globe
with her embrace.

But her shoulders ache. And her arms
are tied. Love is too demanding.
Suspect too.
And hatred?
We abide the question.

Mother India
bleeds with preordained regularity
like the rest of her kind.
To no effect, mostly.
She bleeds as her breed dwindles
even as she tries to grow.

But who can fight the writing
on the walls? The whispers that waft
from ultra sound clinics. Try us,
we can relieve your burden. Eliminate
awkward, redundant commodities
with the most consummate of ease.

Try us. Stop worrying, Mother India,
We'll get rid of
the bleeders/breeders,
for your salvation. Save
your money too.

Because, Mother India,
your shoulders
are not yet broad enough
to bear the weight of your daughters.
So, Mother India, play the numbers game
and sleep easy.

Her Toil, My Toil

She regards me with wonder
Or is it scorn?
I – the diligent screen gazer
inscriber of arcane symbols
to what intent
she wonders no doubt.
Her brisk broom has a purpose
I must relinquish my chair
interrupt the fecund flow of my words.
She needs to sweep beneath the desk
banish dirt.
That's essential toil.

Thoughts on a Ritual

Tracing yellow lines
On broad banyan leaves
Winding the fragile thread
Round and round...
My thoughts
Vagrant butterflies
Take flight...

Savitri…
Constant wife
Faithful lover
Woman of power
You conquered death
Yet…
Your womb was too narrow
It could only hold
A hundred sons
Not a single daughter…

Menopause

There is little to compare
with that sensory knockout
the aroma of a chapatti
roasting on a hot flame
bloating to the roundness
of a mature woman's breasts
just before they begin to sag

Only,
while I was busy measuring out my life
in hot chapattis
providing sensory bliss
I became too absorbed in my task
to notice that the rejected ones
had piled up in stacks to wall me in
like another Anarkali
who exuberantly sought her own doom.

Stale, cold chapattis,
no longer appetising
Too tough beneath my crumbling teeth.

Third Daughter

Uncelebrated your birth,
yet joy blooms
in the tendrils of your hair,
deepens the dimples
in your petal cheeks.

Eager you burst forth
riding the tides of pain.
Unbidden, unsought.
Your coming a song,
enchantment...
A burst of light,
an avalanche of thought.

I have given suck…
felt the dagger of love
twist, sear.
Felt the heat of the star
that draws you
out of the labyrinths
where darkness compresses.
Straight be your flight,
little blossom,
cleave the sky
arrow-sharp
arrow-swift.
Buoyant the winds
that carry you,
wherever
your wish takes you…

I am a Woman

I am a woman
I am soiled paper rupees I am shining gold coins
I am a diamond of glass I am an emerald of paste
a handful of earth flung on the highway
by a contemptuous gardener as rubies course through my veins
and the salt of the sea irrigates the timbre of my voice
a sea deep beyond any submarine's reach.

I am soiled paper rupees in the vegetable vendor's pouch
keeping company with scraps of tobacco.
I am shining gold coins nestling in the bridegroom's lap
waiting to be sold.
I am a diamond of glass glittering in the ruler's crown
maintaining his gloss.
I am an emerald of paste in the queen's necklace
awaiting the evaluator's frown.
And the salt of the unfathomable sea irrigates
the timbre of my voice
producing a song too deep for the shallow framework of words.

I am a handful of earth thrown on the highway
and inside me the seed seeking silence crouches
sheltering from the clamour of the earth.
Then
pushes forth again, bearing jewels
to brighten kingdoms of toil.

I Will be Myself

When you played,
swam
splashed
in the water of my womb,
safe
from want and desire
longing and need,
anger and lust
did you not wonder
as you fought your way out
how you would survive
a water being
on arid earth?
Or, did you bear
your own fulfilment
clenched in your tiny fists?
As you announced
through that first insistent yell –
I am here, I am I,
call me what you will,
I have already chosen the shape of my nose
the sound of my voice.
And
I will be I
in spite of you
in spite of yours
Mother father
brother sister
I will grow and be myself
against all odds!

For Sonali on Her Graduation

Bubbling up,
you grew
inch by inch,
year by year
not overnight maybe,
like Jack's magic beanstalk
but far enough
to reach the clouds
discover the giant's treasure
and carry it back bravely.

Laughing...
you reach out now.
Stretch your arms wide
to take the whole world
into your loving embrace.
Child...
may you always step lightly
on the thorns
life scatters in your path
your light footsteps
lift you far.
Defying gravity
may you float
on a gentle breeze
cool, flower scented
far, far above
this heavy earth...

A Forest of Narcissus

A forest of narcissus
she said,
grew behind my house
this modest seeming woman.

My thoughts congealed like the shimmer
of long ago frost
transforming the ordinariness of grass blades
as I inhaled the forgotten perfume
of small precise blooms
that scented a winter room once
within the whiteness of secure walls.

A forest of narcissus
she said,
grew behind my house.
So many small heads
that had loved themselves to death
in that self-obsessed forest,
yet their fragrance lingered.

Losing

Summer means listless days
struggling to find breath
in the indolent rhythm of card games.
Shuffling, dealing,
the eager grab, the troubled frown
should I call the trumps?
And the eventual
triumphant smack of the winning hand
on the table.
The superior smirk on the winner's face

You play with what you have
What you get
And if you lose
it's only a game of cards
you think.
But already you are getting
adept at the art of losing.
Cultivating the careless shrug
the helpless self-deprecatory smile
the sporting surrender.

It's only a game –
and everyone loves a good loser.
You are loved
And you live in the gloating knowledge
Of toiling for a cause greater than yourself
Allowing others to win,
so generously
when the thunder blast of an unexpected win
flattens your heart beat

you cower
the winner's frown feels like a death sentence
you stare appalled at the treacherous cards
that betrayed you, turned you traitor
interrupted the safe rhythm
of the listless summer days

the afternoon siesta
is no longer dreamless oblivion
but a tangle of nightmares
And
you can never pick up your hand again
with the same cheerful indifference
the confidence of the loser
Because
the winner's cross weights you
and summer
has lost its meaningless sorcery.

Childhood

Childhood Rain

Rain in childhood
falls without explanation
simply pouring out of the sky
we do not dance in it (like my children will one day)
but don raincoats and unfurl umbrellas
stoically set out for our Saturday evening walk.
hand in hand
two by two
a twisting navy-blue crocodile
creeping between two green slopes.

One stretches upwards
draped with silver sheets which reach down
like Rapunzel's hair inviting us
into the castle of the sky
the other tumbles down
into a shrouded sea, daring us to
surrender to its shadowy embrace.
The navy-blue crocodile wriggles on
postponing the moment of decision
waiting for the sun to shine and the mist clear.

A Child Reading

A child reads a book
Innocently, unaware
of the raw danger of words
of the risk posed by meanings
still to be painted
into blank outlines.
Of images to be shaped.
Enchanting images
that inexplicably lose form
falling around her like a collapsed house,

Patience, child
in time, the rubble will be cleared
You will emerge from the dark
confront sunlight
blinking, but your eyes will open again
to clarity.

How Hard to be a Child!

How hard it is to be a child
swaddled in the glossy, spangled satin
of your mother's hopes!

little girls tripping the light fantastic
keeping time
to Mamma's plaintive, imploring rhythm
skating on the thin ice of Papa's love
stretching to seize the crown
that remains a hair's breadth
out of their reach.

Boys dangling from parachutes
negotiating the freeways of the air
aching for solid ground
gulping the hard pellets of
scrunched up screams,
hoping that
soon there will be relief
the reassuring thump
of Papa's back slapping
and Mamma's chortling applause.

How they hope!
Oh...how they hope...

The Highway of the Ants

In the middle of the laughing, shrieking playground
a silent network threads a pattern
through the straggling grass.

It's the ants.
They have trampled a path
a finger thick highway for themselves,
an exclusive thoroughfare
gouged out by countless pinhead feet
assiduously scurrying.

Imagine, minuscule frames I could balance
on the edge of my fingernail
have done this,
shipping loads many times their size
a random grain of rice,
crumbs from a carelessly munched biscuit,
waste that will feed
dozens of them.

Industry
that has snipped an almost invisible ribbon
through the playground.
A ribbon of toil
amidst the devices of leisure,
noiseless striving
amidst the laughter of swings and slides and see saws
barely visible, but present all the same
present, like the narrow path of words
I dig each day
with my striving pen
transporting
the load of thoughts that weighs me down

but must be placed somewhere
to offer possible sustenance
a ribbon of meaning
minute, almost invisible
but sometimes floating into the sight
of an intent observer
marking its presence
like the highways of the ants.

The Gentle Wolf

On my first day of boarding school
I met a wolf.
Seven years old and bawling shamelessly,
I met a wolf.
The wolf rescued me
from my tears
when she pulled me into the warm circle of hands
she was chopping at.
Here I cut, here I break
Here I eat my wedding cake...
Her hands lost their force when she hacked at mine
reminding me, I was a new girl
whose tears had not yet dried.

We shared chocolates and jujubes on Sundays
and together we searched for God.
As we knelt in the chapel every day at break
repeating HailMaryfullofgracetheLordiswiththee
Blessedartthouamongwomen. HolyMaryMotherofGod
Prayforus sinners.
Longing for God to come save us.
Forgive our sins.
Release us from our human frailties,
kneeling on the gravel
savouring its punishing bite
the sharp edge of a flagellation that might make God relent.

But every night it was the Devil
who stalked me,
despite the protection of my Guardian Angel
despite the magic of Holy Water faithfully applied.

Forehead, chest, left shoulder and right shoulder.
The sign of the cross, a charmed armour.
Still, my nameless sins insisted on haunting me.
Dark splotches like criminal ink
that could not be erased even with the strongest
scouring fluid of penance.

Desperate for salvation, the Wolf shared her dream
with her parents.
The dream to renounce this sinful world
seek redemption underneath the veil
and vanished from my life
in one fell swoop.

And I abandoned my quest,
stopped yearning for God
ignored the blackness of my sins
and shrank the Devil to a grain of dust.

But at night I often wondered
what had happened to my dear Wolf,
whose chopping hands were so gentle.
Did she find God or did she give up?
Did she discover that salvation was a mirage?

Cloistered Girl

Smiling, she dances to her own music
within the tortoise shell
of her fate.
Safe in her hijab,
no risks of late night movies for her
no need of time pass thrills.
Perhaps she carries enough laughter
within herself, to seek it
second hand from celluloid.
She does not question either.
Perhaps she knows what she has,
is more than what she doesn't.

The Road to Wonderland

The road to wonderland
is not easily found.
You may tramp through miles of forest
but the rabbit hole will not open up
for you,
sweep miles of fallen leaves
in futile search,
pick up a spade
dig and dig,
only to encounter
the solid rock of everydayness
that will not move
despite the cultivated heft of
your muscle.

The capricious road to wonderland,
it will not reveal itself
you must wait
till the white rabbit arrives
to show the way.

Even if eons pass
before
the whimsical creature decides to turn up.

Once There was Childhood

Once there was childhood
Distant in time and space true
Now shrunk into a tight hard ball
Like the princess's pea
But still perceptible
beneath the numerous mattresses
the years have piled on it
it stabs my back
with the memory
of a time
when stringing the perfect daisy chain
was the greatest anxiety
and the greatest ambition.

Loving and Hoping

Love, that Flighty Djinn

I would have liked to live forever, within
the opaque glass walls of your love. Seeing the world
through misty eyes. The sun's heat
softly tempered to my back. The rain,
a distant, soothing patter. Not a drenching torrent
churning rivers of mud and slime
to drown in. But
the mist holds demons. Their cries
will not be stilled. And glass is fragile
Even a single stone – carelessly flung
can shatter this sanctuary we built
You and I –
out of the power of our dreams
this vaporous castle
which can stand –
only till the magic lasts.

Loving, my faltering steps take root
reaching, touching
my heart, a wing, a feather
caressing you. All night…
your warmth filling me. Battling
the shuddering dark
that waits, a patient, hungry dragon.

But…
love, that timid bird
that flighty djinn. Comes
to roost only when it wishes
Not in response to my call
or yours
No matter how urgent the need
No matter how desperate the hour.

In the Time of Mango Blossom

In the time of mango blossom
pain stabs,
a pale spear
sharp as the scented spikes
that weight the tree
as eager
breathless,
it awaits
fulfilment.
The yearly ritual,
the time of fruit.

Our time was a flower
that bloomed
and withered again.
But –
the seed remained,
dry, insignificant
almost unseen.
And yet –
it held promise
of life
of blossom.
Colour, fragrance
within its husk

The thoughtless wind
tears the flower apart,
scatters its petals.
But
the seed rides its back.

A Dream of Khajuraho

In the pensive hour
before the break of dawn
when nothing is heard
but the music
of worship
my thoughts fly to Khajuraho
and your promise...

Years and years ago
you said
I will take you to Khajuraho
where even stone hearts throb
and love
is permanently enthroned

The years sped by
I waited
for Khajuraho,
waited to visit
the shrine of love
which you said existed
carved out of rock
as permanent as life,
as real as death
as tangible as ourselves...

The years sped by
and
I went to Khajuraho
several times
but only in my dreams...

I stood and gazed at the celebration of life
feeling strangely left out
and yet…
a part of it
as I watched
gods and goddesses
men, women and beasts
permanently entwined in the dance of life
as much as I was
as much as we were
in our own way. Miles
and miles from Khajuraho
the shrine I never visited.
But which lived on
not merely in my dreams
not merely in our dreams
but solidly in stone
as permanent as life
as real as death
as tangible as ourselves.

My Heart a Writhing Fish

My heart, a writhing fish,
on the sands of your silence,
waits
for the firm hand
that will push it back
into the waters that lap
softly
against your barren shores.
Touching, they cannot irrigate
that dryness.
Like a sieve
your sands cannot contain
the water of love.

The tides come and go
spend themselves on the shore.
Leave their flotsam and jetsam
like this poor fish,
my heart.
For how can the water-dweller know
that it cannot survive
in an arid clime
where there is no movement,
where a parched stasis
bogs souls
in a morass
too distant from the waves
that can carry you
as far as you would wish to travel.

Over the Edge of the Earth

You and I
slipped
together
over the edge of the earth
and chose to drop.
Free falling.
Falling free,
holding captive the stars
dancing in our eyes.
The firmament our domain,
our bodies growing
endlessly
till space
could not contain us.

But...
could not resist gravity's pull
and touching earth
we shrank once more
into our mortal mould.
Turned small and limited
once again.

Your Knifing Look

When morrow's need
invades today
sucking the marrow
throwing the bones away
for dogs to bury
and dig up at leisure,
that cracking parchment
of my heart contracts.

Skin and bone
flesh and blood.
Only hard bone has permanence
or parchment sere
or lifeless hair
that cannot feel the scissors' slash.
Then why should this
dehydrated vestige of heart
feel pain
when your knifing look cuts it through?

Shah Jehan Said This Perhaps

Traitor!
The Heavenly One beckoned and you leapt to respond!

He has more to offer perhaps,
my poor mortal love cannot compete with heaven
Mumtaz, I can only heap kisses and jewels on you,
grant you the highest place on the throne of my heart
but this pauper's vault is bare
of the treasures
that have torn you from me with their divine allure.

But do not forget that I am
the Emperor of the world:
you may think you have escaped me
leaving this chill corpse behind
to water with my imperial tears,
if only it were a plant I could revive
with this nurturing moisture.

And do not underestimate the power
of the sighs wrung from the heart of a genuine lover.
Or the might
of the Emperor of the World
who can give permanent shape to the tear that coursed
down his royal cheek
freeze it in stone and in history books
and now I believe in the
gawking camera lenses of wonderstruck tourists
marvelling at the power of love.

The Cage of Memory

The Past is a Foreign Country

Like you,
I too have a past,
a foreign country of my own
whose language I struggle to decipher
flipping through an obsolete dictionary
some of whose pages have been ripped out
slashed with blades, surgical or otherwise
blackened with the soot of fires
ritual, murderous or suicidal
stained with hair oil
blood, guts,
or simply milk, spilt and wept over.

Questions remain unanswered
answers remain unquestioned
argument is stilled with acquiescence
and at the end,
a great weariness
because it has to mean…
it must have been
it's gone, it's done
after all, whatever it was
it happened
in a foreign country.

Once I Had a Father

When I was young and had a father
like any other child… I
clutched his hand. Walked
by his side. Hung on his smile
watched the crow's feet fan out
from the ends of his eyes.
Felt love
a velvet cushion
a tight roof against the rain
a warm hand to hold
and melt the ice of fear
But one day –
the roof blew off
the hand grew cold
and nothing was left
but leafless trees
stretching wan fingers
that tore at my hair
as I walked through the darkness. The bell
tolling in my ears constant…insistent.
The moon, a dented globe.
Washed out, spreading
rancid, milky light
that filled my mouth with sourness.
I heard the sound of weeping
and wailing.
White walls of grief
arose about me.
Smelt fresh earth
felt the horror of
clods

hitting him. Boxed in wood
lifeless, true. But I shuddered
to think of the clods hitting him.
Later, woke on my own, nights
airless, feeling the weight of the earth
squeeze out my breath
engulf, absorb me into itself
Earth, mother
what makes you so hungry
so desperate to swallow me whole?
Digest, ingest
make me a part of you again?
I that would walk on air
and water.
Resist your pull
live on forever
freely riding the wind. Not
bogged down in earth bound clay.
Live till the day when
the grave will empty
and he, they, will come forth whole again
when mud, when clod
will yield forth
flesh and blood
bone and hair
breath and laughter.

A Pearl Within an Oyster

There is a place
where jewelled cobwebs
dot the hillside
my father's smile
never wavers
and the rocks
feel solid beneath my feet.
The mist swirls in the valleys
a potent sea
spewing stories
which my brother
conjures out of the vaporous void.
A magician
spinning a different web each day.
And yet it is I
who tell tales now.
Fishing in that timeless sea
of the past
finding
old shoes
a rotted corpse
but sometimes
a pearl within an oyster…

Misplaced Sounds

1

A girl with naked eyes
sings
at my window
a song
only I can hear
a song
that the wind
gathers into its wide apron
and funnels into my reaching ears
which do not need a hearing aid
like my mother's
did
like my mother
whose world grew small and secret
as it grew still and soundless.
Each day
the birds withdrawing their music.
Each day
sound shrivelling like a dying seed,
as she watched faces frowning,
as she watched faces smiling,
and each day
she frowned and smiled
along with them.
Along
with the fleeting memory
of the renegade sounds
that had escaped the labyrinths of her ears
to prowl like vagrants
on the highways of the air.

2.

The whistling thrush trills no more
as it dips its turmeric coloured beak into the puddle
below the garden tap.
The tap
has vanished along with the sounds
that fled my mother's ears.
Vanished along with my mother
who followed those sounds.
There's nothing but dust where it stood
and there's nothing but dust where she stood.
And black as the granite that holds her memory
is the void beneath the water tap,
black as the glistening thrush's wing
is the void that has eaten up its music.

3.

But
a girl's voice
still
floats across the dark waters
rides the air waves naked as day.
Sharp
as the unheard song
that echoed in the abandoned labyrinth
of my mother's ear,
and
somewhere...
my heart beats so distant,
yet its whisper stamps itself on my page.

The Ghost of Christmases Past

1.

One day, Papa said, he decided
to give up cigarettes. From forty a day,
he came down to none. Only
on Christmas Day,
when the swarm of visitors has diminished
to a select few
sipping their rum in the exhausted drawing room
does he pick up a Capstan Navy Cut
from the carved Kashmiri box
and blow smoke rings for our delight.
While a lonely piece of cake
sits on a chipped plate
surrounded by indifferent crumbs.

The Big Day has not ended we know,
we have yet to negotiate the rocky path
to the brightly lit room
where Santa Claus will distribute gifts
for a price:
poems squeezed from reluctant minds
mimic songs that have long forgotten their tune.
But I cannot, I will not parrot 'Daffodils'
not even to earn a gift. Rejected, it lingers
under the Christmas tree,
another lonesome participant in a festive rite
lies there accusingly as I lurk sullenly in the shadows.

Ishwar chho mero gwalo
kai baate ki kami raunli
The Lord is my shepherd

I shall not want.
but I want, I want, I want
an unconditional gift, Lord
from the night which sucks up fading carols
and flings them among
the silent pines. Already
a ghost, Christmas is slipping away
searching for its past,
amidst the cake crumbs, gift wrappings
and the cigarettes in the carved Kashmiri box.

We will smoke them my brothers and I
alone on New Year's Eve
we will blow foetal smoke rings
aborted by choking coughs
which drift heavenwards to join
the Christmases gone. And
the New Year arrives, stamping in on frozen feet
singing,
Ishwar chho mero gwalo

The Lord is my shepherd,
I shall never want, I hope
for unconditional gifts.

A Gathering of Bones

The bones scattered on Flanders' fields
are being gathered, I hear, a century later
and my throat clogs with unexpected emotion
Contemplating those countrymen,
strangers true,
yet men whose memories
fragmented like their bones,
toll a familiar knell.

Weary boots that marched stoically in an alien cause
the bayonets that slashed an incomprehensible arithmetic,
guns that stuttered a message
the perpetrator could barely grasp.

What stern imperative drove them?
what helpless need?
what stories did they live and die?
what bonds strain and snap
along with their bones?

And my wayward thoughts loop to another time
another war, as irrational.
My father.
My own father
negotiating a surge of bodies
a chorus of groans
staunching the flow of blood
Indian and foreign
stitching, setting, closing gaping eyes,
swollen tongues seeking a drop of ganga jal
homeless spirits suspended in distant territories
for eternity.

My father, resisting the gleam of black market gold
to embrace the warm glow of integrity
returning with an honest
but flawed fortune
that slipped through his fingers like blood
from a mortal wound that cannot be staunched
because money too can drain away
wastefully into the indifferent earth.

Leaving behind only the enemy's sword
whose provenance we never cared to probe
when we could
nor the meaning of the revolver under Papa's pillow
the origin of the bloody kris
that someone shattered,
uncaringly turning a relic into a game of darts
erasing the fragile legacy that curved within its
zig zag blade.

Were those ridges actually speckled with dried blood
or was it venom?

Thus, do family ties snap
deceptively invincible
yet brittle as that blade of memory.
And many a time
no space remains for remembrance
or commemoration
no time to grieve for the blood
that flows in separate streams
never to mingle again.

This River

No boats ply on this river
whether to ferry people
or rescue them.
Never have and never will
only the flimsy boat of memory
skids over the rocks on which we perched once
Over the multihued pebbles
we reached for with delight
clucking with dismay
when they turned drab in our hands.

This river…how we raced through the dim forest
to reach it
eager feet unconscious of the miles
we traversed to gaze upon
the indolent flow that embraced the smoothness
of once jagged stones it had been patiently
polishing to the roundness
of a mother's nurturing breast,
for centuries perhaps.
Sometimes indolent, yet rushing at times
with unseemly haste,
sometimes pausing
as if to plumb its own depths,
This river.
Did it know its own capricious mind?

How dreamy the afternoons we spent,
lounging on its rocky shores
blinking at the hoard of diamonds
the careless sunshine strewed on its ripples
the warmth of its waters massaging our feet.

Only once we exclaimed
at the relentless greed of the millstream
that seized my small brother's

toy crocodile
and swept it away to some unknown destination
before our helpless eyes.

That was just a plastic toy snatched
from a frisky child.
But this river took what it wanted
when the mood came upon it.
It had never nurtured a crocodile
in its murky green depths
only insidious, invisible whirlpools
that turned a father's beard white
drove him from the town
when he could no longer bear to drink
to bathe in those waters
the waters gushing from his taps,
seemingly blameless,
but in truth, tainted
with his young son's dying breath
the same mundane waters
that had lured a boy
into their deadly embrace
when an afternoon's sport
became fatal indulgence.

And we, as we tramped home of evenings
through the fast darkening forest
shivering at the jackals' ominous howling
the sudden hoot of an owl hastening our step
the humdrum chirping of the crickets
scraping our ears like a portentous chant,
we never gave a thought
to this river, that this sun specked river
could deal out death, even as it quenched our thirst.

This whimsical river of my childhood
that never held a boat on its rocky breast,
Never could and never will.

I Little Knew

When
I opened the door
for you to walk out
I little knew
how large was the space
within me
that you had filled
with your careless laughter
thoughtlessly spent over unnumbered hours.
Little knew
how long the road
you would traverse.
How distant the climes
you had to seek
following your star…
And I remained
rooted
congealing
shrinking
while the space around me
grew beyond all reach.

Through the Looking Glass Darkly

Once...you have been
through the looking glass
darkly. Glimpsed that secret self
that lurks
within the convoluted crevices
of your mind. Hidden deep
behind that tamed beast
your everyday self
that dutifully describes the motions
of your very ordinary life.

Once...you have heard
that unheard music. The siren song
of the counter world
floating in the abyss. Too dark
too deep
for any sun to penetrate, let alone illuminate.
Unlocked unseen doors
with invisible keys.
Can you come back? Climb up
the weary ladder to reality
having filled that jewelled serpent
with the dull opiate
that will keep it somnolent, safe
for another century perhaps. A hundred years
of oblivious solitude. Disdaining
that world so real/unreal
which waits with its sad magic
too beautiful to contemplate
spurning its unbearable rapture
for the cup of tea at seven

breakfast at eight
lunch dinner. A telephone constantly shrilling
car wheels spinning
eternally
whirling you on and on
till the clock stops…
And that priceless treasure
hidden
behind the looking glass
remains unspent…
only
because
you could not dare
to look upon the face
of that terrible beauty. Embrace
the dark wonders
that dwell behind the looking glass…

Cityscapes

Every Morning, Every Night

Every morning, Neruda
I see blood flowing through the Delhi streets.

Bodies crumpled like paper bags
to feed a giant incinerator.

The sparks fly upward
plant themselves in the sky
glow Mars-like.
Busy feet
demolish the wisps of ash that escape.

Every night,
I see water rising through the streets.
Home lies somewhere I know
among
those islands that drift like lost cattle.
If you can get to it
negotiating the hours worn threadbare
as lascivious rubber mouths
mercilessly chafe the tarmac.

Rain glistens like a skin of sweat
on the city's dark arms
Blood continues to flow
like wine turned to water.

Good Thoughts

In the uncharted territory of the mind
Where thoughts rove unrestrained like outlaws
There exist too
Little settlements of polite
Well-mannered people
Correct thoughts.

Spotless
As a freshly laundered sheet
Uncontaminated by any streak of random grime
the nuisance of bird droppings
or the accidental shame
of menstrual blood.

Thoughts that balance
adroitly on the straight and narrow
tight rope, resist the buffeting of the gale
that seeks to topple them.

How the poor creatures struggle
against disorder
exercise
eat nourishing food
construct forts
forge weapons
against the marauders
unfettered, undisciplined thoughts.

It's hard indeed, for good thoughts
to survive. This is a war that can never end.

When the Lights Went Out

Where were you when the lights went out?
Wrenching the dregs of poetry from a reluctant muse?

Dregs, stale as the tears that dried
long since on the cheeks of a corpse
the corpse whose head parted company
from the body it had known
for barely 27 monsoons.

The body stays its course
not knowing it has lost its head
the head
abandoned beside a railroad track.
mourns the unknowing body
that plunges on, propelled by a momentum
that launched itself long before
the parting of ways.

Light is faster than sound they say
and electricity gives both to thunder
but who ignites
the bombs that send body and head
on separate journeys?

Who separates poet and muse?

Seven Lives

Tomorrow hovers
like the bridegroom, breathless
at the prospect of seven lives
of conjugal bliss.

But each murky fibre
winding through trembling palms
is yet to be unravelled
palms that bunch like laundry bags
camouflaging their tell-tale tracery
of ineffaceable grime.

Palms that reach for arcane patterns
that might offer more permanent camouflage
than the bridal henna
too transitory to navigate
seven lives of hoped-for conjugal bliss.

Streetlights string garlands
of ancient gold
and car horns trumpet like
the elephant transporting the bridegroom
through the night
towards the avid eyes
the bodies stacked like plates
at a buffet.

Celebrating, darkness throbs relentlessly
keeping company with the festive crunch of bones
the cheery tinkle of smashed glass.

Capitulates with a sigh
as veiled in bridal red
tomorrow arrives,
sudden and startling as a screech of brakes.

Graciously, night suspends itself
so that someone can embark at last
on the odyssey
that tediously insists on
spanning seven lives
with eyes wide open
in daylight.

Words

Words like Pine Seeds

Words
let loose on the air
like pine seeds
lofted by playful summer breezes
that coax them from the mother cone
as she opens her womb
to free her offspring,
despatches them
to seed another world,
new and hopefully brave,
sends them to launch pristine forests
to perfume the air
and whisper arcane secrets all day.

But lost, forgotten
when a plundered kernel
strays to lose its sweetness
squanders it on a gluttonous tongue.

Its taste might linger
like the memory of tearing
gossamer wings apart
the expectant crack that yielded
a momentary sliver of joy.

But how minuscule the guilt,
of forests consumed
before they could sprout?
How brief the regret
for words cast by the wayside?
words

plump with promise once
compelled to dissolve
into the non-substance of memory.

Yet sometimes, persistent as echoes.
Persistent as the aftertaste
of long consumed pine seeds.

Poetry Calling

Poetry's voice
that had seeped like rain water
into the earth
merged into a distant aquifer
sneaks back onto newspaper pages
reminding me that it's alive and thriving
even if in subterranean passages
hidden from my sight.

The confused day searches
for the right words
to fill moments that gape
whitely
for words that no longer exist
except
as a few grey strands of memory
tangled in a broken comb
like an unbending finger that will always resist
the gleam of gold.

Not like a Mango Seed Sprouting

When words will not sprout
Like the mango seed of your childhood
The seed you buried with hope and doubt
The seed that astounded you with
Its wizardry of green
Emerging from mundane soil
Tender, fresh
Trembling like victory unfurling

When words refuse to emerge
congeal in your throat
like unshed tears
entombed in the clutter of daily living
that accumulates like garbage on city streets
choking the eager mango seed
Not even a stout broom can help

Only an iceberg advancing through the mist
To plummet you into chilly depths
Can force you to burst from the depths
fighting for air
propelled by a force beyond you
Much like a mango seed sprouting.

Breaking the Sound Barrier

Naively, poetically
so many things can be said.
Unheard of things. Non existent
tongues emerge, find voice. Words
spout from sewed-up mouths
that never possessed articulation
but now miraculously acquire the
gift of the gab. And
you listen astonished, as
gibberish suddenly sorts itself out
to make almost geometrical
patterns of sense.
Q.E.D.
Only
they do not intend to demonstrate
a point, maybe. Have no logic to prove
only seek the freedom to let their
particular brand of sound loose
from its ancient cage.

Sound that is burgeoning
shaping its forms with such
unseemly haste that it cannot
but distend its receptacle,
that fragile wall of flesh
to bursting point. Burst to
shatter the barrier of sound with
such a deafening boom
that everyone is compelled
to give ear.

Compelled to pay heed
to the naïve rhythms
of newly born poetry. Surrender to
the sorcery of sound
hibernating for eons.
But awakening now with
a yawn of thunder.

Poems like Butterflies

Poems like butterflies
that will not linger long enough
for you to grasp.
Poems fleeting as the flash
of lightning
that the camera of your mind
cannot grab entire in their brilliance.
Poems like pebbles
multihued under water,
fading like a rainbow
the moment you pick them up.
Poems like dreams abandoned
when daylight corrodes
night's alchemy to dross.
Poems carelessly trodden into the dust
like flowers discarded by a deity

Poems, weeping like a lost child
forsaken.

Unexpected Poem

Today I opened the door
and a poem slipped in
she did not ring the door bell
she never does
she did not smile in greeting
she seldom does
with wrinkled brow
and eyes heavy with sleep
she stepped in, slow and sluggish

but she was a poem
and I embraced her with savage joy.

Wayside Poetry

I scented the elusive fragrance
long before a helpful breeze blew it in
through a crack in the window,
The window bolted, sealed against
The pollution of the world outside.

How had I forgotten
that the grimy motes of particulate matter
the colonies of teeming germs
are the seeds of poetry?

The over wise innocents
playing cards on the wayside
pausing to rap on your car window.
Their reality
obliterated by your fear
as you clutch your purse
and your branded cellphone.
Repulsed by the practised note in their whining
the dust in their dishevelled hair.

A scant traffic light later,
dogged by guilt and regret
myriads of schemes race through your mind
competing for attention.

In the end you just mail the cheque
Someone will take care of them, you hope
And every night you give thanks
for the warm softness of your bed
the solid walls that shelter you

the sealed windows
but
poetry drifts in to remind you of
their world-weary eyes.
Wayside poetry.

A Poem is a Strange Thing!

A poem is a strange thing.
Sometimes
exploding into life
whole, complete, perfect as a newborn babe.
Sometimes
carefully cut to measure
like a garment
lovingly crafted
embellished, embroidered
and proudly worn.
Sometimes
an abscess
burgeoning, suppurating
then bursting open
to spill its pain
for all to view.
Sometimes
a skeleton
festering in one's cupboard
till it's brought out
to face the sharp cold glare
of friendly faces
who cry,
so –
this is what she has been hiding all this time!

Stillborn Poems

1.

Stillborn poems
forgotten fetuses
lie in the dustbin
unmourned, like girl children.

2.

The songs that never were,
wander in the ether
and the blood that never flowed
congeals in the gutter

3.

Men made of sticks
march across pages
And cardboard trees
reach out for cellophane skies.

4.

Battles that will never be won
burgeon on TV screens
While the defeated whimper
in wastelands far from home.

Random Utterances

The Train to Nowhere, The Train to Somewhere

The one who has to come will come
the one who has to leave will go away.
I cannot choose, they say. It
has all been written, they say.
The words chosen, the path mapped.
The time of arrival, the time of departure
and you must wait on the platform
not knowing when the train will arrive or depart.
Or where it'll take you.

There will be no announcements
true or false
about its arrival or its departure
but nothing will stop you either, from
supping a leisurely cup of tea. Or
one so hasty that it scalds your tongue. Stop you
from sharing a joke with the stranger who perches on her trunk
or from browsing at the book stall
poring over titles. Turning
a desultory eye on the pictures that illustrate a tome,
even imbibing some fleeting textbook wisdom.
Or from
buying a book you'll leave behind on your seat
when you disembark. For the next traveller to enjoy or deride,
perhaps. Or for the beggar
who'll enter the vacant train in search
of the scraps that remain
mute testaments of your last meal. The
empty water bottles that will fetch a few coins.

The book might be sold for scrap
or its pages lovingly turned.
What difference does it make?
The words were not your own. As
you thought when you read it.
Someone else had chosen them.
So what if they seeped into your mind and became yours.
The words were the writer's. The
one who writes all our lives
Not yours, hopeful reader.
And perhaps
when the train stops and it's time to disembark
knowledge will streak through your mind
like lightning illuminating the evening sky
and you will realize they were always there,
floating in the wind
unseen microbes, biding their time.
waiting for the fogged microscope of your eye
to clear and find them.

While countless trains came and went
describing endless journeys to God knows where.
Then you will learn
it matters not who the writer is or who
the reader. It is enough that words exist
those golden grains gleaned out of the mind's dust
to nourish a famished moment.
And when this knowledge confronts you
as you step off the train
you have everything and yet have nothing.

The words and the book
the music and the song
you have them and you leave them
with no regret
or sense of loss.
Because they will not be orphaned
as you once feared.

Another will claim them, nurture them.
Another who paces the platform
waiting to mount the train.
Not knowing the time of its arrival or departure
not knowing its final destination
yet eager for the journey which promises
everything and nothing.

Cape of Good Hope

Hope there always is – always should be
Even
when a ship is being smashed
against the rocks. There is hope.
Despite the frailness of the sea tossed plank
that might possibly bear you
safe to a rocky beach.
And hope is always good.

Hope, white as the foam of breakers
effervescing as they batter rocks
with amorphous power
pulverising them
into the softness of sand
yielding, formless but permanent.
How far can you reduce matter?

Somewhere
not too far beyond the Cape, colours
blend and separate
as alien waters meet. Let go
and meet again
in a never-ending embrace.
While the indifferent waves pound
the rocks in ceaseless battle.

The lighthouse
keeps silent, solitary watch.
Its sweeping eye
perforating the thickening dark
with its blinding gleam of hope.
Hope that is permanently good.

Palm Sunday

You were not unaware
of the efficacy of the grand gesture.
The triumphant entry,
a torrent of palms swirling in the air.

But how did those welcoming fronds
transform themselves to scourges?
Heaven alone knows perhaps,
Heaven, who spawned those Siamese twins
agony and ecstasy,
knows that triumph is a crown of thorns
bloody footprints mark the path
that leads to the ultimate elevation
in the company of thieves.

Yet, the grand gesture survived.
We still wave palms transformed into crosses
commemorate your death
and celebrate your rebirth.

The Graveyard has Shut me Out

I cannot be laid to rest
like Rilke
in the earth I have chosen
for my own burial.
That much is certain, for
the graveyard has shut me out.
Not for me the dreamless sleep
beneath benign deodar trees, which stretch
tireless arms, sifting
sunshine and rain.
Not for me the granite gravestone
preserving my name,
modest cenotaph
an idle stranger might wonder at,
the way I have mused over Sarah Elizabeth
and Baby Mickey.
Sure, I will become dust and ashes too,
but nameless dust flung far from the walls
of a beloved graveyard,
walls that shut me out
growing higher
each time I attempt the leap.

Collateral Damage

Assiduous worm
tirelessly spinning your shroud of silk
unmindful of the death plunge.
Spinning, spinning
like a suicide bomber
priming himself for glory
the rainbow sheen of that fragile capsule
the bubble of reputation.

Are you sure that life's just for dying,
and death for living eternally?

Your silken shroud gleams
ephemeral as a wayward
wisp of sunlight that glimmers
just long enough to show up
the motes of dust in seemingly
pure air. Ephemeral as smoke
merging into darkness. And even
while the collateral damage
orbits the earth boastfully
your glossy shroud is snatched
away for someone else's glory. Leaving
nothing
but the shrivelled worm-corpse
flung by the wayside
for birdfeed.

No Way in

That bird,
that silly creature
trying to peck its way in
through the glass barrier
of my window pane. That
bird brain, just will not
understand. There's
no way in.

You just cannot walk
or fly in wherever you wish.
There cannot be free movement
everywhere. We have to protect
ourselves from small minded
visitors like this bird. There is
a protocol to be followed. You
need to approach through
the correct entry points. Properly oiled
channels on which the heavy doors
can move smoothly to let you in.

Bird brain. The glass pane
is much stronger than your
skinny beak imagines,
pecking so helplessly.
And don't try to get a claw
in the door by claiming that
you like the look of my face
and would like to come in

to cheep your appreciation
in person. Such sycophancy doesn't
impress me. What can you offer
but dry wisps of grass or the
wretched worms you dig up
with such zeal? Only, if
like a jackdaw, you can locate
a precious jewel, I might consider
opening the door,
just a crack.

Flowers they are Simply Amazing

Flowers, they are simply amazing.
They can bloom everywhere. Nod
sedately beside my patch of lawn,
spread luxuriously on the grass on the hillside,
even astonish an arid desert with their wanton colours.
They can waft their scent through my window
as they wind around a pillar
working their way up to the sky perhaps,
where no doubt they will turn into stars.

Sometimes they spread themselves beneath my feet
ornamenting a carpet. Or
wrap themselves around me
brightening the kurta I carelessly pluck from my cupboard.
Sometimes they alight on the cup from which I sip tea
or nestle on my daughter's gleaming locks, containing
a wayward curl. They
have even been known to march up the walls of a room
or engrave themselves on a box of wood or marble.
Bejewel a necklace, an earring, even a bracelet,
disembodied, they squeeze their essence into a perfume bottle
or scent the sighs of a desperate lover.
Flowers they are simply amazing
they turn this mundane world into a magical garden.

Robben Island

Another place of the skull
Another Golgotha
Clean neat bleached to the bare
necessities of existence
belying the flagrant thrust
of arum lilies
blooming in random clusters.
Extravagant trumpets
large, full blown, secure in their whiteness
rooting themselves where they will
unlike the baby penguins
huddling in bushes
before our alien onslaught

The wind outlines the bleakness of the sun
as a silent prison
willingly unlocks doors
and secrets flutter free.
Dues paid
the toiler in freedom's mill
is now permitted the luxury
of endlessly reliving hunger and pain
anger and hate.
While courteous hordes
listen
wrestling with what and why
and who and which
and right and wrong
wondering how deep
they might insert their
delicate probes

beneath the armour of calluses
How deep burrow
before their dentist's drill
encounters the unguarded nerve

In the end
one thinks
he has a tale to tell at least
and eloquently too.
If not would hasty bank notes pile
up on the dignified palm
eager to repay someone else's debt?
To buy absolution for another's crime?

In the end
what remains
but the naked skull of truth
even a free man needs to eat
and the heat of youthful rage
cannot flame far enough
to disperse the chill of age.

The wind is curiously dry
as we sidle away from the limestone quarry
thanking God for the good karma
that kept us secure in distant climes
for the screen of designer glasses
that saves our eyes
for the watered milk of human kindness
that did spurt at last from skull dry breasts
while the black coated penguins
carefully measure their mincing strides
earnest as lawyers arguing a case
lost long before they crawled out of their eggs.

The ocean shimmers all the way to the mainland.
There are drinks to be sipped on the ferry
the wonderful wildness of wind on your face
the curio shops beckon
and Mandela's smile soothes.

But somewhere we know
a man waits
smoking a quiet cigarette
outside the dispossessed prison
waits for the next bus load
for the guilty caress of notes
on the expressionless palm
whose lines have bound him to Robben Island.

Old Eyes

Old eyes
tire easily,
seeking lost treasures
in a maze
of words that blur on pages.
Dog eared, well thumbed
too thumbed
like oft shuffled memories
that crumble like worn paper.
How exhausting the burden of years
of lines
annotated in a language
that has changed too many hands
turned obsolete, anachronistic
become truncated like
songs stripped of music
faded as a much-washed sari
or the taste of once coveted delicacies
whose flavour
is as faint now as the stain
of careless tea that dripped on a page
washing out the words.

In the Park

Laughter booms like frantic guns exploding
in the eager park. Plangent with hope,
restless with movement. As desperate potbellies
wage futile battles and weary sticks stump
determinedly, burying that monster age. That
stalks even the lissom bodies that speed past
muscles rippling, precious breath escaping to join the clouds.

The bemused trees watch, thicken their own
girth with indifferent ease.

Chants hammer the air beat demons away
and khaki knickers flare in the discipline mode
present obedient arms to barked commands
prepare for battles still loitering in distant corridors
like snipers awaiting their moment.

And – all the while
an inexorable needle slides on
describing endless rounds.

Clouds embrace and part
the sky darkens and clears
light flutters like a trapped bird
finally accepts its bondage within the grey dome.
And one by one the seekers vanish from the park
boarding buses and cars, departing to chop onions
push pens or computer keyboards (more battles waged
more skirmishes fought/lost/won)

While the complacent trees thicken slowly
nurturing their roots with their own leaves
giving and taking, giving and taking
as the needle pushes insistently on
always taking, never giving.

To Emily Dickinson and All Those who Write Unheard in Seclusion

Long ago a bird sang
a hidden bird
smothering her song
containing its sweetness
within her own heart
like a cool stream
quietly flowing
beneath the earth
content to be.
Not caring
if the sun
touched it with its long fingers
lent its light to transform
stray specks of its being
into diamonds to dazzle
the jaded world.

She bid her time
while her jewels hardened
found their own light
and shone out
independent
of the whimsical sun.

Solitude

There's something about
four walls and myself
uninterrupted silence
barely felt thoughts
laughter caught
framed and hung on a wall
sometime long ago.

Nothing stirs the air
around my head
no alien thoughts
no alien needs
clashing against my will
only
me, me, me,
filling the emptiness.

No vacuum this –
this self contained space
but a singing laughing
fullness, expanding, spreading
unrestrained.

Where is Glory Better Sought?

When I have finished irrigating the country's soil with
my fertile blood. Seeding new warriors.
I will turn into fodder for famished screens. Millions of my faces
will bloom upon the idiot box
increase, multiply and feed countless starving eyes.

My blinded gaze will face compassion boredom
horror terror sympathy and disgust
my 15 seconds of fame glide across the microscope's glass
and evaporate before the arc lights' glare
as gyrating limbs and thumping breasts
overtake my fleeting image and
leave it far behind.

What race is this I lost before it began?
or did I win it standing still? Watching
my opponent's heels kick nakedly at the oncoming dusk.
Synthetic dusk born from the smoke of guns
as irrational as my night which lingers on and on
while indolent dawn snuggles beneath the covers
waiting for someone else to switch on the light.

But. Where is glory better sought
on green grass or in slime?
facing the gritty winds of summer
or winter's shroud of fog?
which does blood stain brighter
desert sand or mountain snow?
And. Who lights an eternal lamp for me
as I float, an anonymous cloud
carrying the rain child of glory in my womb
a child which refuses to be born
till the storm settles.

A Fish's Life

I had hoped for another tomorrow
Not the one
that beckoned with hooked fingers

my scales sketching fleeting silver crescents in the air
sickles without any useful edge
I danced, I danced
But there was no getting away
The hook has dug deep, holds me tight
And my silver has a tired gloss
As I become one with the charcoal evening

The perfidious river pleats into cautious ripples
Draws the darkness deep into itself

Obliterating the memory
So many caught
So many yet to be caught.

The Clouds are Moving on

The clouds are moving on
Like indolent sheep
Sauntering through an azure meadow
Thanks for making space for the sun, clouds
There's washing to be dried
Dishes stacked away
And beds made in chilly rooms

The clouds are moving on
like time serving sheep
seeking better pastures
it might rain somewhere else today
thirsty fields receive a
long awaited drink
someone will welcome the relief
from a blazing sun

The clouds are moving on
Like wisps of cotton fraying
To the fine core of fibre
Dissolving in the sapphire sky
Soundlessly
The meadow is gobbling up the sheep
While the benign sun beams at the sight

Only a single brush stroke of cloud
Stretches now like a falling star
Searching for a safe landing
Will this fledgling survive the meadow's onslaught?
Who knows?

Interrupted Clocks

Many clocks have interrupted themselves in my house
Bad vaastu I'm told
Bad feng shui too, no doubt
But this is a dilemma anyone might face
When
There are too many clocks in the house

In some the batteries are too spent
To push the seconds into minutes
Minutes into hours
The needles too worn out to measure time
Others have more complicated problems
Innards so screwed up by accident or age
That even the most adept clock healer
Is lost for a cure

All the same, they continue to hang on the walls
Nestle dustily on shelves and desks
Keeping faith with moments that have stood still
For months or years

But twice a day at least
For a fleeting minute
These interrupted clocks
Are not out of sync with time
Like any of us
they have their useful moments.

Imaginary Snows

You will have to imagine the snow mountains, the man said,
They are there, somewhere above the horizon
I tried to,
aching to lose myself in the old enchantment,
I groped behind the dingy grey curtain
that separated me from the mountains
yearning for the blessed sheen of a vision
unfairly snatched from me.

Breathless with hope, I riffled through the clutter of memories
stacked like curling old photographs,
strained to locate the blue backdrop
Against which they had glistened so carelessly once,
Distant, I knew
yet close in their angled whiteness
Embracing the sun with jagged arms
Pouring its brilliance back into my dazzled eyes.

I tried to imagine them, the beloved mountains,
washed a purposeful pink at dawn
Glistening pristine white at noon
and drowsing under the molten glimmer of dusk.

of course, they were there, somewhere
beyond the limited range of my sight,
somewhere behind the dingy curtain we had dragged over them
the grime of polluted breath, the soot of corrupt smoke
the dust stirred by indifferent vehicles.

they were there even if I could not see them,
like beautiful women cloistered to evade
lecherous gazes
they dreamed their secret dreams
shutting me out.

I did not doubt that they were there,
in a space beyond my reach.

But, what if
the lens of memory fogged over?
Imagination was not enough
And you began to wonder,
Did the snows actually exist?
Or had they poured themselves away
Into the restless mud of the torrents that rushed past
Swirling, boiling?
No longer serene and unmoving
Rooted and secure
pristine-white, firm as belief?
What then?

Mirrors Cracking

Every day you hear mirrors cracking
when faces smash beyond recognition
Or is it just masks coming off?
The truth revealing itself when buried thoughts
Rear up as whispers
and whispers turn into shouts
Crowding the air
clamouring on paper and sprouting on screens
drowning out everything else.

History was always a story
that could be retold like a folktale
To suit the dominant narrative
and we make new discoveries afresh
When heroes transform into villains
Because it is time to strip off the masks
And let the buried truth emerge
be shared, be multiplied a millionfold.

Gandhi, your spectacles have been crushed
under the heel of a new millennium
Trampled over and over again
your vision cannot be recovered.
It cowers somewhere in a subterranean shelter
Like a shell-shocked child.
There is no space left anywhere now
For experiments with truth
Because the truth today is a rock,
implacable, immovable.
There is no room to experiment.

On the Top of a Mountain

To stand level headed
On top of a mountain
Is a worthy feat, I know.
To stand at the summit
And gaze clear eyed at the drop below
There are days when fog
Obscures the depth of the abyss
on others, sunshine blinds your eyes
Sometimes it's the echoes that confuse you.
Darkness is the worst.
Then there is the wind
It tugs at your clothes.
You pray that it will not turn into a gale
that will push you off the top
hurl you into oblivion
the furious torrent that inexorably rushes on
At the bottom of the mountain.

Acknowledgements

The publication of a poetry collection is a landmark event for the poet. It is not accomplished without the encouragement of editors of literary journals and support from family and friends. I would like to express my thanks to all the editors who have found enough merit in my poetry to publish it. Much gratitude to world renowned poet K. Satchidanandan for his kind comments and for featuring my early work in the prestigious *Indian Literature*, journal of the Sahitya Akademi – a real boost for a newcomer. Heartfelt thanks to my dear friend, acclaimed litterateur Prof Malashri Lal for her generous and perceptive endorsement. Celebrated poet Sukrita Paul Kumar, another old friend, shared insightful comments and valuable advice and I am extremely grateful to her. Warm thanks to dear friend Vibha Singh Chauhan, a leading academic and writer, for her discerning observations, and to well-known poet Dr Jaydeep Sarangi for his valuable insights. Mandira Ghosh, Secretary, Poetry Society provided enthusiastic support and played an important role in the publication of this book. Many thanks to her! Hugs to my beloved granddaughter Adya Sharma, who took out time to design this striking cover. Gratitude to my wonderful publisher Sudarshan Kcherry of Authorspress and his efficient staff for their inputs and for bearing with my ongoing changes in the manuscript.

And as always, to my husband Dilip Agarwal and my daughters Garima, Sonali and Geetika: "You are the wind beneath my wings!"

Publishing Credits

Several of these poems have been published previously. "Thoughts on a Ritual", "Anarkali" and "Third Daughter" first appeared in the journal *Manushi.* "Love, that Flighty Djinn", "In the Time of Mango Blossom", "My Heart a Writhing Fish", "Your Knifing Look," "Once I had a Father," "Mother Dominica's Tranquil Square", "Losing," "Tranquillity", "Palm Sunday," and "A Pearl Within and Oyster" were first published in *Indian Literature.* "I will be Myself" and "Over the Edge of the Earth", appeared in *Kavya Bharati.* "This Is Not A Country with Smooth Roads" "She, Innocent Fly" "Ambushed," "The Past is a Foreign Country", "Woman on the Road to Lhasa" "Every Morning, Every Night", "Seven Lives" "Words Like Pine Seeds" "Imaginary Snows" "A Fish's Life" have appeared in the web journal, Museindia.com "Mother India" and "Breaking The Sound Barrier" in *Indian Horizons.* "This River" in the web journal *Teesta.*

Some poems have also appeared in anthologies like *Still we Sing*, edited by Sarita Jenamani, *100 Great Poems for Children*, edited by Deepa Agarwal, *The Puffin Book of Poetry for Children* edited by Eunice de Souza and Melanie Silgardo, *Echoes of Khajuraho* an anthology published by Bharatiya Gyanpeeth, as well as in school textbooks.